# GOODNIGHT HORSEY

## FRANK ASCH

Prentice-Hall, Inc. / Englewood Cliffs, New Jersey

Prentice-Hall International, Inc., London
Prentice-Hall of Australia, Pty. Ltd., North Sydney
Prentice-Hall of Canada, Ltd., Toronto
Prentice-Hall of India Private Ltd., New Delhi
Prentice-Hall of Japan, Inc., Tokyo
Prentice-Hall of Southeast Asia, Pte. Ltd., Singapore
Whitehall Books Limited, Wellington, New Zealand

10 9 8 7 6 5 4 3 2 1

Library of Congress Cataloging in Publication Data
Asch, Frank. Goodnight horsey.
SUMMARY: A request for a bedtime glass of water results
in a fantastic horsey ride with a surprise ending.
[1. Bedtime—Fiction]   I. Title.
PZ7.A778Gp  1981  [E]  81-7332
ISBN 0-13-360461-6   AACR2

To Jan and Devin

Every night before I go to sleep,
my daddy brings me a glass of water.

Then he reads me a story,
gives me a kiss,

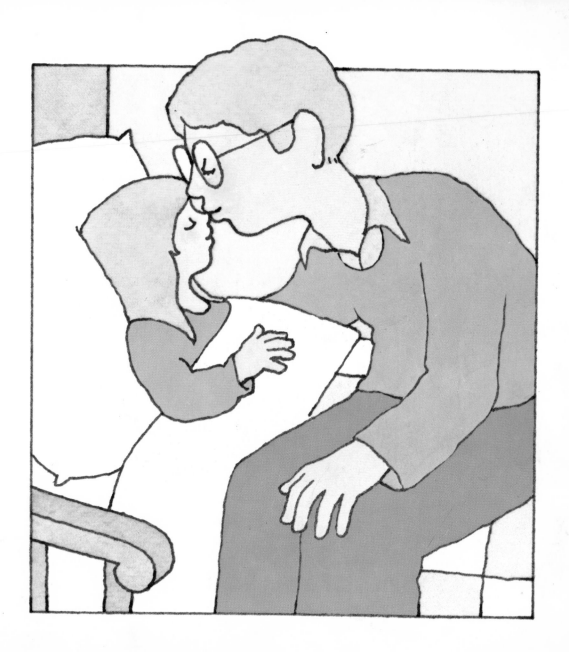

and turns out the light.

But one night before I went to sleep,
I asked my daddy for a horsey ride.

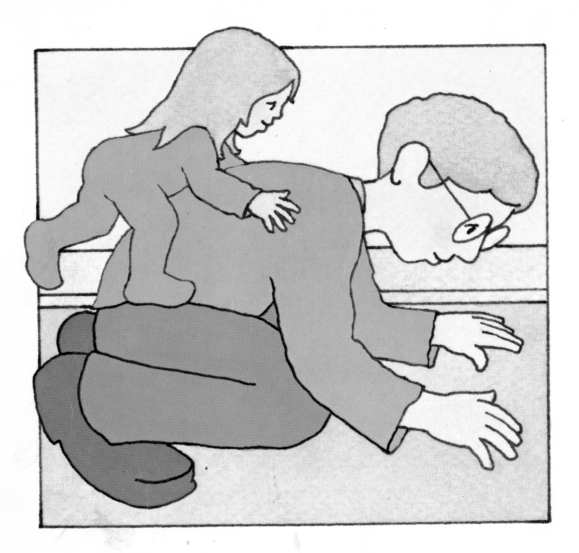

As soon as I climbed onto his back...

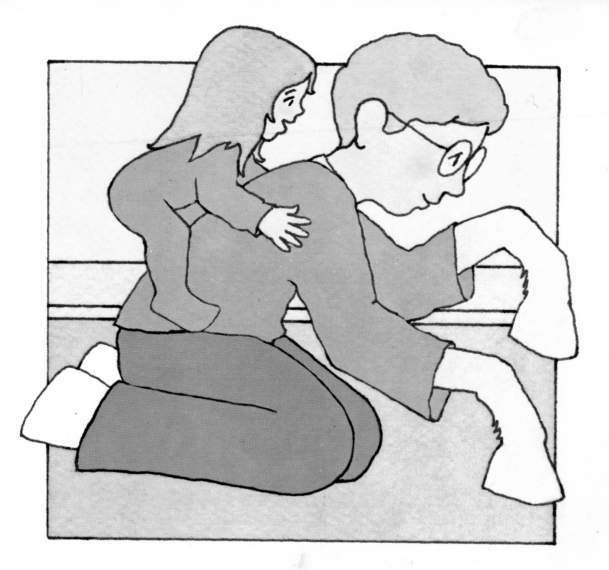

his hands and feet became hooves.

His ears got longer,
and he grew a tail...

just like a real horsey.

And I felt like an Indian princess…

riding through the forest.

"Giddyap," I said, and we galloped

as fast as the wind.

Until the sun went down,
and my horsey said...

"Time for bed."

Then he brought me a glass of water,

read me a story,

and fell asleep!

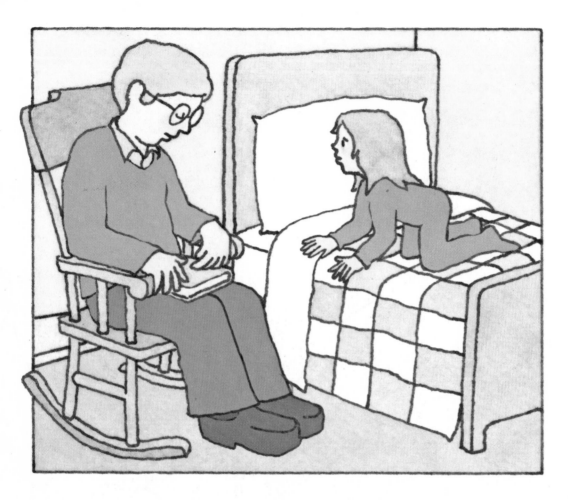

"Poor Daddy," I thought.
"He must be very tired."

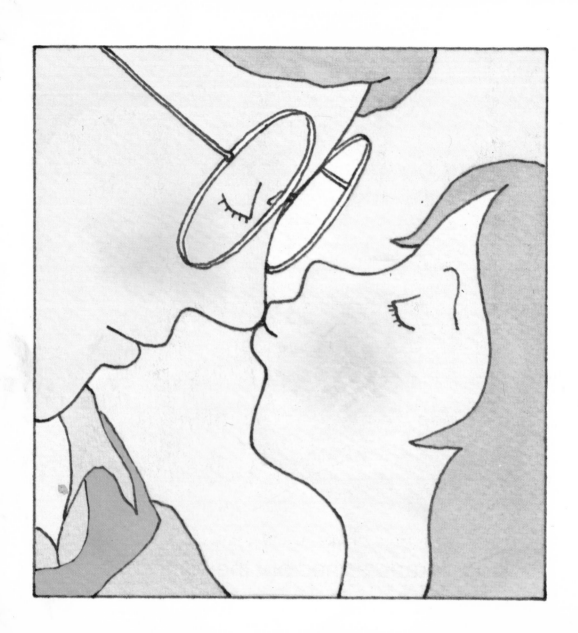

So I gave him a kiss
and turned out the light.

Goodnight.